MONSTER BIRTHDAY

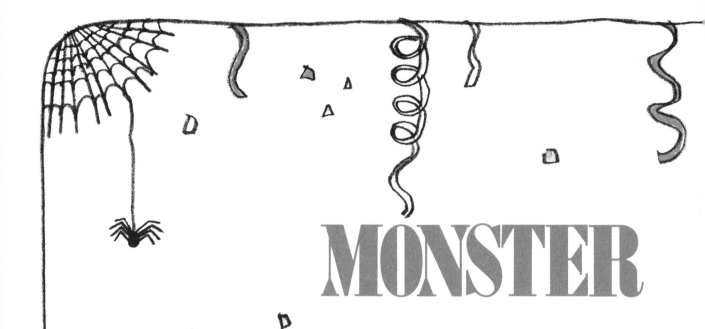

MONSTER

by

illustrated by

Holiday House

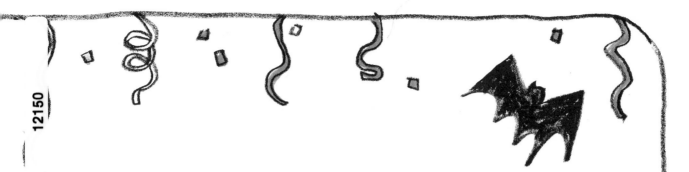

BIRTHDAY

Steven Kroll

Dennis Kendrick

New York

For Joan Daves, agent and friend

Text copyright © 1980 by Steven Kroll
Illustrations copyright © 1980 by Dennis Kendrick
All rights reserved
Printed in the United States of America

Library of Congress Cataloging in Publication Data

Kroll, Steven.
  Monster birthday.

  SUMMARY: Muck the monster reluctantly attends his
friend Slug's birthday party.
  [1. Monsters—Fiction. 2. Parties—Fiction.
3. Birthdays—Fiction] I. Kendrick, Dennis. II. Title.
PZ7.K9225Mo   [E]   79-16203
ISBN 0-8234-0369-6

When the invitation came to Slug's birthday party, Muck said he wouldn't go.

"Why not?" said his mother. "Slug's one of your favorite friends."

"I don't like birthday parties," said Muck. "They're too messy."

"Monsters are supposed to be messy," said his father.

"Well, I'm not a messy monster," said Muck, "and besides, I'm too shy."

"Slug's feelings will be hurt," said his father.

"All right, I'll go," said Muck, "but I don't know what to give her."

"Why don't you give her a dinosaur balloon?" said his mother. "You know how Slug loves dinosaur balloons."

The day of the party, Muck walked very slowly over to Slug's house. It was windy, and the dinosaur balloon was hard to hold. Muck also wanted to be late.

But he wasn't. He reached Slug's house at the same time as his friends Pig, Mess, and Goo. Goo went up the steps and rang the doorbell.

Before anyone could answer, a gust of wind swept the dinosaur balloon out of Muck's hands. It flew up and up and into a tree. Suddenly there was a loud POP!

The door flew open. "What was that noise?" Slug shouted.

Muck burst into tears. "Your present!" he sobbed. "It was your present!"

"Don't worry," said Slug. "Come on in and enjoy the party."

Slug's parents had put slime all over the living room floor. There were cobwebs hanging from the windows. Leering lanterns dangled from the ceiling. Dust was piled in the corners. Rats and lizards were stuffed between the sofa cushions. Mice and bats were hidden under the rug.

The monsters wasted no time. Goo caught three rats and a lizard. Pig rolled himself up in the rug and nibbled on mice and bats. Mess and Slug stamped around in the slime and swung from the curtains. Everyone rolled in the dust and caught spiders. Except for Muck, who hid behind the sofa.

Then it was time to open the presents. Pig's was a jar of onion perfume. Goo's was a box of monster eyeball marbles. Slug dropped the box. Marbles scattered everywhere. The monsters chased them until they'd turned over all the furniture. This time Muck had to hide behind a door.

Mess's present was a monster doll. Slug hung it from a hook on the ceiling.

"I'm going to keep it there forever," Slug said. "It will remind me of you."

"Cake!" shouted Slug's mother. "Ice cream!"

Mess, Pig, and Goo raced into the dining room and sat down in the snaggletoothed chairs. Slug sat at the head of the snaggletoothed table.

In the middle was a gigantic birthday cake with seven
monstrous candles.

"Go to it!" said Slug's mother. "Make as big a mess as
you want!"

Everyone sang "Happy Birthday" to Slug, and poured sticky punch on her head.

Slug made a wish, and blew out the candles. Before she could cut the cake, Pig started to grab it. Bits and pieces of cake and ice cream flew across the room.

The monsters shrieked. They rolled around on the floor and stuffed cake and ice cream into their ears and noses.

"Hey," shouted Goo, "where's Muck?"

Muck was hiding under the table. Mess and Pig dragged him out. They stuck cake and ice cream in his nose and hair.

"Hey, Muck!" shouted Goo. "You look thirsty!" And she threw punch in his face.

Poor Muck. He rushed to the bathroom. He tried to wash himself off. This party was turning out to be worse than he thought.

When he got back to the living room, everyone was ready to play Pin-the-tail-on-the-monster. Slug's mother put on the blindfolds. Slug's father gave each monster a tail with a thumbtack on the end. Then they all spun around—and went after one another!

But no one could find anyone else. Pig plunged his tail

into the wall. Goo stuck hers into the sofa. Mess and Slug bumped into each other, and set off in different directions. No one could find Muck because he was back behind the sofa.

Slug tripped over a chair and landed on the slimy floor. "Let's play Heads instead!" she shouted.

All the monsters except Muck gathered in a circle.
They ran at one another and butted heads. Everyone sat
down hard on the floor except Slug.

"I win," she said.

"It's your birthday," said Mess. "You should win."

Then they dashed upstairs to bounce on the beds. They ran so close to the sofa that Muck stepped back. He didn't want to be found again.

His foot touched something hard. He jumped—and turned around. A lizard stared up at him. He'd been stepping on its tail.

"Good afternoon," said the lizard. "Percy's the name.
You don't seem to be having a very good time at this
party."

"I'm not," said Muck. "I hate it."

"I might say I agree. Do you think we could leave

and do something else?"

"I don't think so," said Muck. "I really should stay. Slug would hate it if I left."

"Well," said Percy, "perhaps we can remain on the sidelines a bit longer."

Together, Muck and Percy tiptoed up the stairs. The monsters had already broken Slug's bed. Now they were jumping on her parents' bed.

"I'll race you to the banister!" Goo shouted.

The monsters poured out of Slug's parents' room and tumbled down the banister on top of each other. They ran into the back yard, dug up lots of dirt, and threw it around. Then they raced around the house five times, trampling on the flowers.

Muck and Percy watched the rumpus from a window.
"You know," said Percy after a while, "I think they've

forgotten all about you."

"You know," said Muck, "I think you're right."

They left the house by the front door. They hurried
away down the street.

"Percy," said Muck, "would you like to come over to my house?"

Percy smiled. "Why of course," he said, "as long as it's not your birthday!"